D0908481

Lana Lynn
Howls at the Moon

To Deanna and Rollo and the black sheep that they raised
—*RVS*

To Emanuel, whose sense of adventure inspires me
—*AS*

Published by
Peachtree Publishing Company Inc.
1700 Chattahoochee Avenue
Atlanta, Georgia 30318-2112
www.peachtree-online.com

Text © 2019 by Rebecca Van Slyke
Illustrations © 2019 by Anca Sandu

Edited by Kathy Landwehr
Design and composition by Nicola Simmonds Carmack
The illustrations were rendered digitally.

Printed in January 2019 by Tien Wah Press, Malaysia
10 9 8 7 6 5 4 3 2 1
First Edition
ISBN 978-1-68263-050-1

Library of Congress Cataloging-in-Publication Data

Names: Van Slyke, Rebecca, author. | Sandu, Anca, illustrator.
Title: Lana Lynn howls at the moon / written by Rebecca van Slyke ; illustrated by Anca Sandu.
Description: Atlanta : Peachtree Publishing Company Inc., [2019] | Summary: Lana Lynn is not content doing what the other sheep do, so one night she dons a disguise to run and howl with a pack of wolves.
Identifiers: LCCN 2018032052 | ISBN 9781682630501
Subjects: | CYAC: Adventure and adventurers—Fiction. | Contentment—Fiction. | Sheep—Fiction. | Wolves—Fiction.
Classification: LCC PZ7.1.V39 Lan 2019 | DDC [E]—dc23 LC record available at *https://lccn.loc.gov/2018032052*

Lana Lynn
Howls at the Moon

Written by Rebecca Van Slyke
Illustrated by Anca Sandu

PEACHTREE

ATLANTA

Lana Lynn was an intrepid sheep.
The other members of her flock were
content to nibble grass in the pasture,
sip water from the pond,
or nap in the meadow.
Lana Lynn wanted more.

Lana Lynn wanted adventure.

She wanted to run through the wild woods.

She wanted to stay up late.

She wanted
to howl at the
moon.

The others thought Lana Lynn was an odd sheep.
"Lana Lynn, come nibble some grass," said her
best friend, Shawn.

"Fiddle-dee-dee! Grass is tasteless! Not for me,"
said Lana Lynn.

"Lana Lynn, come sip some water,"
said Shawn.

"Fiddle-dee-dee! Water is boring!
Not for me," said Lana Lynn.

"Lana Lynn, come take a nap. I found the perfect place," said Shawn.

"Fiddle-dee-dee! Naps are dreary! Not for me," said Lana Lynn.

"You are an odd sheep, Lana Lynn," said Shawn.

That night, as the flock dozed under the full moon,
Lana Lynn tossed. She turned. She tried counting sheep.

"Tasteless grass, boring water, dreary naps," she said.
"Fiddle-dee-dee! I want adventure!"

So off she went.

She tiptoed past Shawn and the other sheep, who were sleeping soundly. As she passed the shepherd's hut, she noticed a strange, hairy blanket tacked to the wall.

"The perfect disguise," she said, and she slipped it over her head.

Lana Lynn dashed into the wild woods.

"This is the life!" she shouted as she ran.

But Lana Lynn was not alone in the wild woods.
Yellow eyes watched her as she ran. Pointed noses
sniffed the air. Sharp teeth grinned at her.

She skidded to a stop.

"Hello," said Lana Lynn.

"Hello," said the biggest wolf. "You must be new to these woods. Come run with us."

"Golly gee! Running wild? That's for me!" said Lana Lynn.

Lana Lynn and the wolf pack ran through the wild woods.

They stayed up very late.

They howled at the moon.

As the sun rose, the biggest wolf said, "We want you to come back to our cave with us. For dinner."

Lana Lynn was hungry for some nice grass. She was thirsty for a sip of water. After a long night spent running through the woods, she was ready for a nap in the meadow.

"Fiddle-dee-dee!" Lana Lynn yawned. "I'm
exhausted. Not for me."
The wolves circled around her.
"Oh, but we insist."

Mama Wolf had dinner waiting for them at the cave. "Have some squirrel," she said.

"Fiddle-dee-dee! Puny squirrels? Not for me," said Lana Lynn.

"Have some rabbit," Mama Wolf said.

"Fiddle-dee-dee! Scrawny rabbit? Not for me,"
said Lana Lynn.

"Then have some sheep!"

"Shawn?" said Lana Lynn.
"Wana Wynn?" mumbled Shawn.
Lana Lynn looked at her friend.

Running through the wild woods, and howling at the moon may be fun, but it doesn't make me a wolf, she thought. I'm still a sheep. And this cave is no place for a sheep.

"Golly gee! I love sheep! That's for me!" said Lana Lynn, grabbing Shawn. "I hate to eat and run," she called as they ran out of the cave.

"That new wolf is very greedy," said Mama Wolf.

"But she is lots of fun," said the biggest wolf.

Lana Lynn and Shawn ran all the way back home and collapsed in a heap.

"I'm glad you weren't nibbling grass in the pasture or sipping water from the pond or napping in the meadow," Shawn said.

But Lana Lynn did not answer.

She had nibbled some grass and sipped some water. Now she was fast asleep in the meadow. She looked like a very contented sheep.

"Fiddle-dee-dee," said Shawn.

But whenever the moon is full, an intrepid new
wolf runs through the wild woods again, staying up
late and howling at the moon.

Because even a sheep likes a little adventure now
and then.